6/11/03

Rehder

To Joann Wheeler,

Thank you for teaching.

God bless your work!

Pam Alexander

A. Fischer.

# Yumion Goes to the City

Written by:
Rhonda Frost Kight

Illustrated by:
Pam Alexander

Volume II

The phrase "Be Sweet" is in the illustrations 6 times throughout this book. If you can find them all, you are a true "sweetie."

Dedicated to our children
Jason, Ruby, Rachel, and Leeanna

Special Thanks

To our Lord Jesus Christ, who began a good work in us and will be faithful to complete it.
Philippians 1:6

To Fisher Barfoot, Tommy Irvin, and Zell Miller for their contributions to this state.

To Pruet, who taught me to love words and helped me find the right ones for this book.

To Jean Kunold, who led us through publishing with kindness.

To all of the children who helped Yumion accomplish his mission.

Text copyright ©2002 by Rhonda Frost Kight
Illustrations copyright ©2002 by Pamela M. Alexander
Printed in the U.S.A.
All rights reserved.
First U. S. Edition 2002

Yumion™ used by permission from the Toombs-Montgomery Chamber of Commerce
Vidalia Onion® used by permission from the Georgia Department of Agriculture
Coca-Cola® is a registered trademark of The Coca-Cola Company
Pre-press performed by Colson Printing Company, Valdosta, GA
Printed by Quebecor World Book Services, Kingsport, TN
Published by Be Sweet Publications, Inc., Collins, GA
Website: www.besweetpublications.com

When we last left Yumion, he was leaving his home
to tell the world about onions from St. Simons to Rome.
He'd proclaim the state secret that was born in his town.
He vowed that he'd travel roads up and then down...

The man looked Yumion over from his stems to his shoes,
smiled proudly and said, "Sure, I'll tell you my views!
I'd start in Atlanta under the dome of gold.
And this is the message they should be told:

The Brown Thrasher, Live Oak, and Cherokee Rose
are symbols that every good Georgian knows.
Your name would make that list more complete;
you should be the state vegetable: The Vidalia Sweet!"

Yumion knew Mr. Barfoot was telling him true,
for the fellow seemed to know just what to do.
He pondered a moment and said, "Thanks a ton!
I must run along now, there's work to be done!"

The driver said, "Hop on, you big ol' onion!"
His rider said, "Thanks! By the way, my name's Yumion!"
The man said, "I'm Raymond! Hang on tight won't you please,
'cause up there you're bound to get quite a breeze."
"Yahoo!" Yumion said, as he looked forward and grinned.
"I'm off to the city!" he yelled into the wind.

The truck drove into the State Farmers Market, and they looked around for a place they could park it. Yumion thanked Mr. Raymond and ran toward the gate; he was so excited he could hardly wait!

He roamed the aisles of peanuts, squash, and tomatoes.
He walked among apples, pecans, and potatoes.
A variety of foods that each appetite savors;
all kinds of colors and all types of flavors.

Finally he spotted some kids who were walking,
so he went over to them and he began talking.
"Can you help me?" he asked, being very polite.
They answered the stranger with a kind, "We might
be able to help if we know what you need."
Yumion smiled and said, "You're good friends indeed."

"I'm going to the capitol building of gold,
and there are ways to get there, or so I've been told.
I'd be very thankful if you could give me a tip
about the best way to continue my trip."

One boy said, "A bus will be your best shot.
Some buses go that way, but others do not.
Bus 346 will stop here in a moment;
you'll go to the capitol if you make sure you're on it."

Yumion said, "Thanks!" as the bus pulled up alongside.
He stepped on and braced himself for the ride.
As the bus began moving he saw a sign on the door.
"Oh no!" he cried, "I'm on bus 364!"
"How could this be?" he wondered aloud.
He looked back to see a bus fade in a cloud.

Being a well-mannered onion he thought simply,"Oh my.
I'll just see where this takes me," he said with a sigh.
Just then he saw it, just as he'd been told;
a beautiful flash of a building of gold.
"There it is!" he said as his bus rolled right by.
"How will I ever get back? Oh goodness, oh my!"

The bus finally stopped and Yumion looked up in surprise.
"Where am I?" he asked as he shielded his eyes.
He saw a train going around on a track
and skylift cars going up and then back
from a really gigantic mountain of rock
as big around as a whole city block!

At the train the kids shouted, "Good luck, new friend!
Come back when you have more time to spend!"
Yumion boarded the train with his mission in mind.
He did not expect to be this far behind.
A sweet looking lady searched for a seat,
so Yumion, the gentleman, rose to his feet.
He said to the lady with the smile that he wore,
"Please take my seat. I'll stand by the door."

As the crowd moved Yumion got pushed all around,
and the next thing he knew he was flat on the ground.
They hadn't meant to, but they'd caused him to tumble.
He jumped up and brushed off without even a grumble.

He read **Zoo Atlanta** on a sign overhead.
"Perhaps someone here can help me," he said.
So he followed the people inside to find out
just what this new place was all about.
It was better than he could have guessed:
Lions, gorillas, and birds in a nest!
This was a home for some special creatures,
so he thought he'd check out some of its features.

Signs pointed toward pandas, so cute, black and white.
He headed there first, and to his delight
he caught sight of them there as they were lunching.
It was stalks of bamboo on which they were munching!
"These guys are the cutest fellas around,
but I must get back on track to downtown.
Where to go next and how to get there
is my problem right now, I've no time to spare!"

As he walked in the field the children had shown
he realized something he hadn't known!
Somehow he'd gotten into the rhino's backyard.
Now he'd better keep up his guard!
He jumped in a tree for his own protection.
A helpful giraffe headed in his direction.
"This is a neck on which I can depend.
I'm really glad you have this, my friend!"

The giraffe carried him through a field that was wide,
then lowered its head and Yumion did slide
down to the other side of the gate.
"Thanks!" Yumion called. "Now I won't be so late."

When he saw some kids who were standing right there,
he thought they'd be frightened, but they only stared
at the onion that had landed right at their feet.
Big veggies didn't usually walk down their street!

Around and along with the traffic he swerved;
on some roads he turned, and on some roads he curved.
Yumion kept riding 'til his throat got dry.
He shouldn't stop now but he had to try
to find some refreshments to quench his big thirst.
A dry onion mouth could be simply the worst!"

He wanted a place to get something to drink;
surely he'd find it here as quick as a wink!
Coca-Cola®, he knew, was delicious and yummy.
He couldn't wait to get some of it down to his tummy!

Sure enough, at the very next corner he rounded
a great soda fountain was there and it sounded
like a river running right through the place.
It put a big smile on his big onion face!

Soda flowed freely from every spout.
There were no cups in sight, so he crawled right out
to the fountain with his dry mouth open wide
so that sweet fizzy drink could flow right inside!

He drank until he could hold no more,
he was really refreshed and he jumped to the floor
to find a way out and be on his way.
This had been an exhausting day!

While looking around he began to think,
"There's more to Coca-Cola® than just a great drink!"
He stopped to hear someone nearby tell some history
and he learned that the recipe is kept a great mystery!

He found out that it once sold for five cents
in a drug store fountain to ladies and gents.
It's a product about which Georgia can boast;
it all started here, now it's known coast to coast!

Up the steep steps of the building he bounded
knowing that everyone would be astounded
to meet an onion with a message to bring;
an onion who had many praises to sing!
He went in as though he was expected,
and to his surprise he was directed
to the place where the governor was walking.
Yumion strolled right up and started talking.

## Stuffed Vidalia Onions®

4-6 Large Vidalia Onions®-cored (save middles)
1 can cream of mushroom soup
1 can of English peas-drained
1 jar of chopped pimento
1 lb. block processed cheese
salt and pepper to taste
2 Tbsp. butter


Preheat oven to 350°.
Peel and core onions. Chop and sauté middles in butter. Mix remaining ingredients with cooked onions. Place whole cored onions in a greased casserole dish and stuff with mixture. Put remaining mixture in casserole dish. Bake for 1 hour or until onions are soft. Serve as a side dish.


Lachele Yancy
Winner
2001 Vidalia Onion® Cookoff